BAD DATE

by PJ Gray

Copyright © 2016 by Saddleback Educational Publishing. All rights reserved. No part of this book may be reproduced in any form or by any means, electronic or mechanical, including photocopying, recording, scanning, or by any information storage and retrieval system, without the written permission of the publisher. SADDLEBACK EDUCATIONAL PUBLISHING and any associated logos are trademarks and/or registered trademarks of Saddleback Educational Publishing.

ISBN-13: 978-1-68021-114-6
ISBN-10: 1-68021-114-5
eBook: 978-1-63078-431-7

Printed in Guangzhou, China
NOR/1115/CA21501590

20 19 18 17 16   1 2 3 4 5

Stacy pulls out her phone.
She sends a text to Lena.
Lena is her best friend.

"How was your date? Tell me!"

"Where are you?" Lena texts back.

"Off from work in five," Stacy texts.

"Okay. Meet me **next door.**"

Stacy sells clothes at a shop.
Next door is a burger place.
Lena is in a booth.
She waits for Stacy.

Work is done.
Stacy finds Lena.

"How was your date?" Stacy asks. **"I can't wait!"**

Lena sits there.
She looks at her drink.
"It was okay," Lena says.

"**Okay?** What do you mean? You wanted this date so bad. You said Jeff was hot," Stacy says.

"He is," Lena says. She shakes her head. "I don't know."

"I don't get it. What's wrong?"

Lena had liked Jeff a long time.
They went to the same school.
They had the same friends.
He was good-looking.
He liked her too. She knew it.

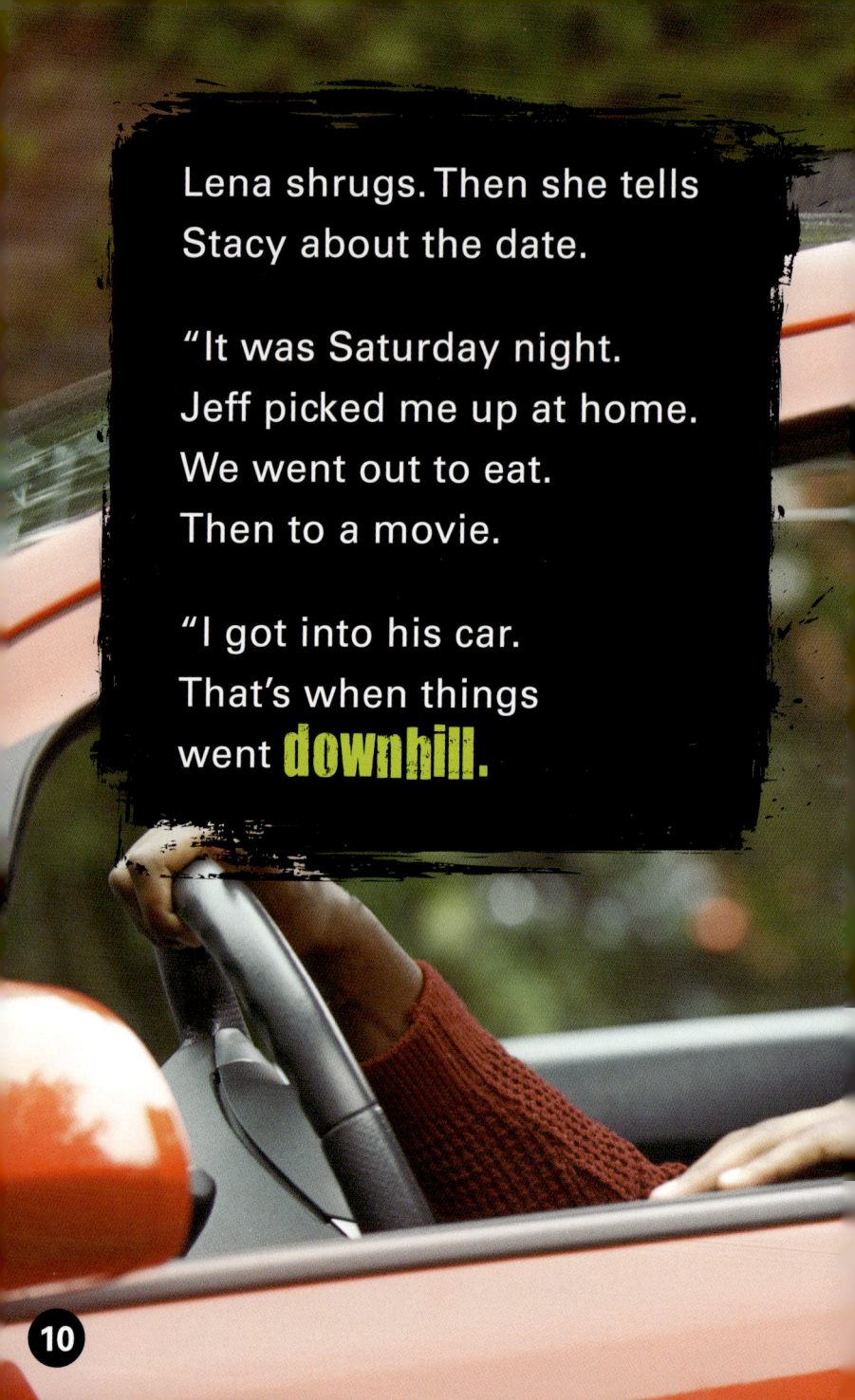

Lena shrugs. Then she tells Stacy about the date.

"It was Saturday night.
Jeff picked me up at home.
We went out to eat.
Then to a movie.

"I got into his car.
That's when things went **downhill.**

"Jeff's car **smelled bad.**
I didn't say anything at first.
I tried to smile.
Jeff kept driving.
He asked me if I was okay.

"I told him his car smelled bad.
Jeff turned red.
He opened the car windows.

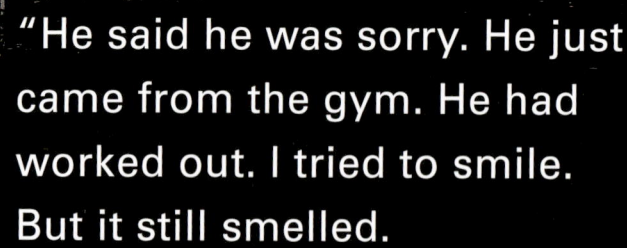

"He said he was sorry. He just came from the gym. He had worked out. I tried to smile. But it still smelled.

"Then Jeff said he knew what it was. He pulled the car over.

"I saw him check the backseat.
He pulled out his
gym shoes.

"They smelled really bad.
I pinched my nose.
Jeff put the shoes in the trunk."

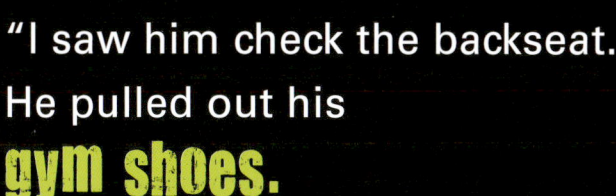

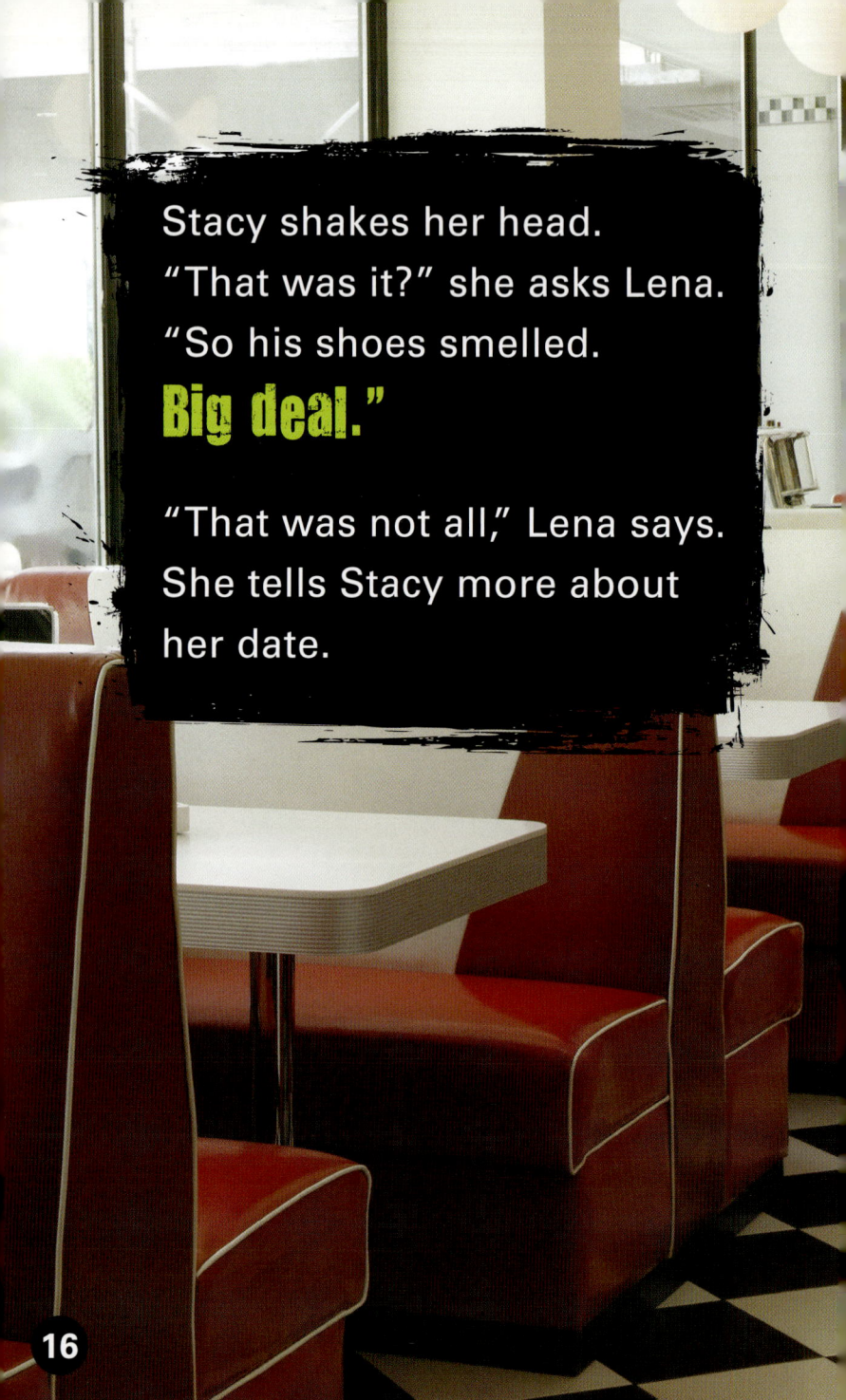

Stacy shakes her head. "That was it?" she asks Lena. "So his shoes smelled. **Big deal.**"

"That was not all," Lena says. She tells Stacy more about her date.

"We went to the movies.
He sat next to me.
The lights went out.
The movie began.

"Jeff moved in.
He put his arm around me.
I was happy.
Then I sniffed.
Something **smelled bad.**
It came from under his arm.

"It was **gross.** I don't think he took a shower.
So I pulled away from Jeff.
I sat back in my seat.

"He asked if I was okay.
I told him my back hurt.
So I had to sit up in my seat."

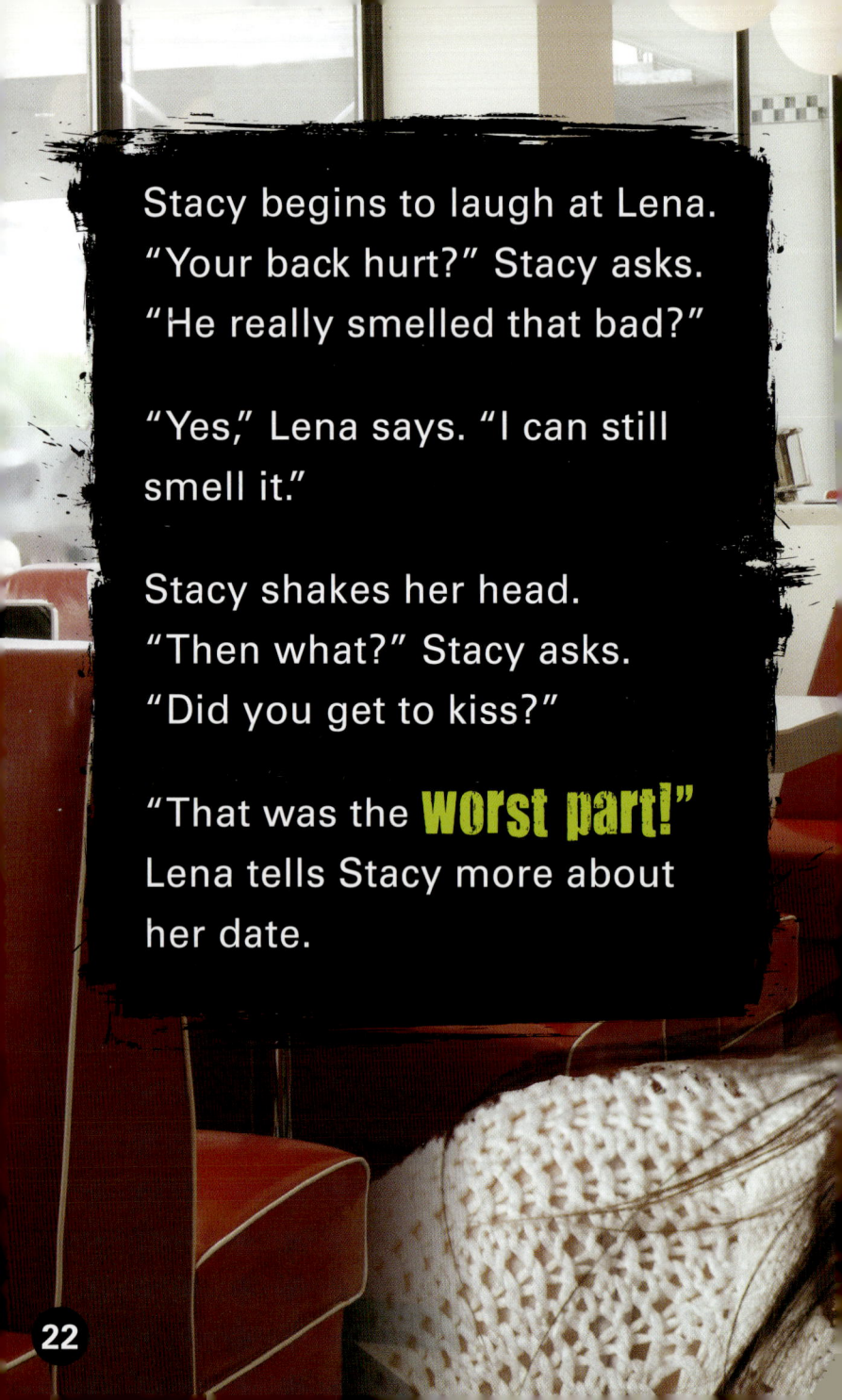

Stacy begins to laugh at Lena. "Your back hurt?" Stacy asks. "He really smelled that bad?"

"Yes," Lena says. "I can still smell it."

Stacy shakes her head. "Then what?" Stacy asks. "Did you get to kiss?"

"That was the **worst part!**" Lena tells Stacy more about her date.

"It was dark.
The movie was on.
Jeff slowly reached for my hand.
We held hands.
He smiled at me.
I smiled back.
It felt **good.**

"We watched the movie.
Then Jeff turned to me.
He asked if I wanted a drink.
I shook my head.
He said he would be
right back. Then he got
up and left.

"Jeff came back and sat down. He had a **hot dog.**

"It had chili and onions on it. Jeff ate it very fast.

"The movie played on. We held hands again. We smiled at each other.

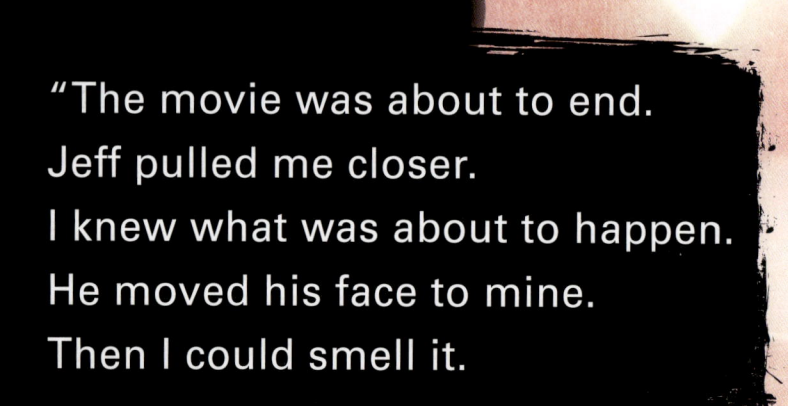

"The movie was about to end.
Jeff pulled me closer.
I knew what was about to happen.
He moved his face to mine.
Then I could smell it.

Onions!
His breath smelled like onions.

"I had no time to think.
Jeff kissed me.
But I pulled back."

Stacy shakes her head.
"No! Not **bad breath!**"

Lena nods her head.

"And that was it," Lena says. "He took me home. I shook his hand in the car. I got out of the car fast. Then I ran into my house."

Stacy begins to laugh. "That is so sad," she says. **"And funny."**

Lena's face turns red. "Shut up!" she says. Then Lena begins to laugh too.

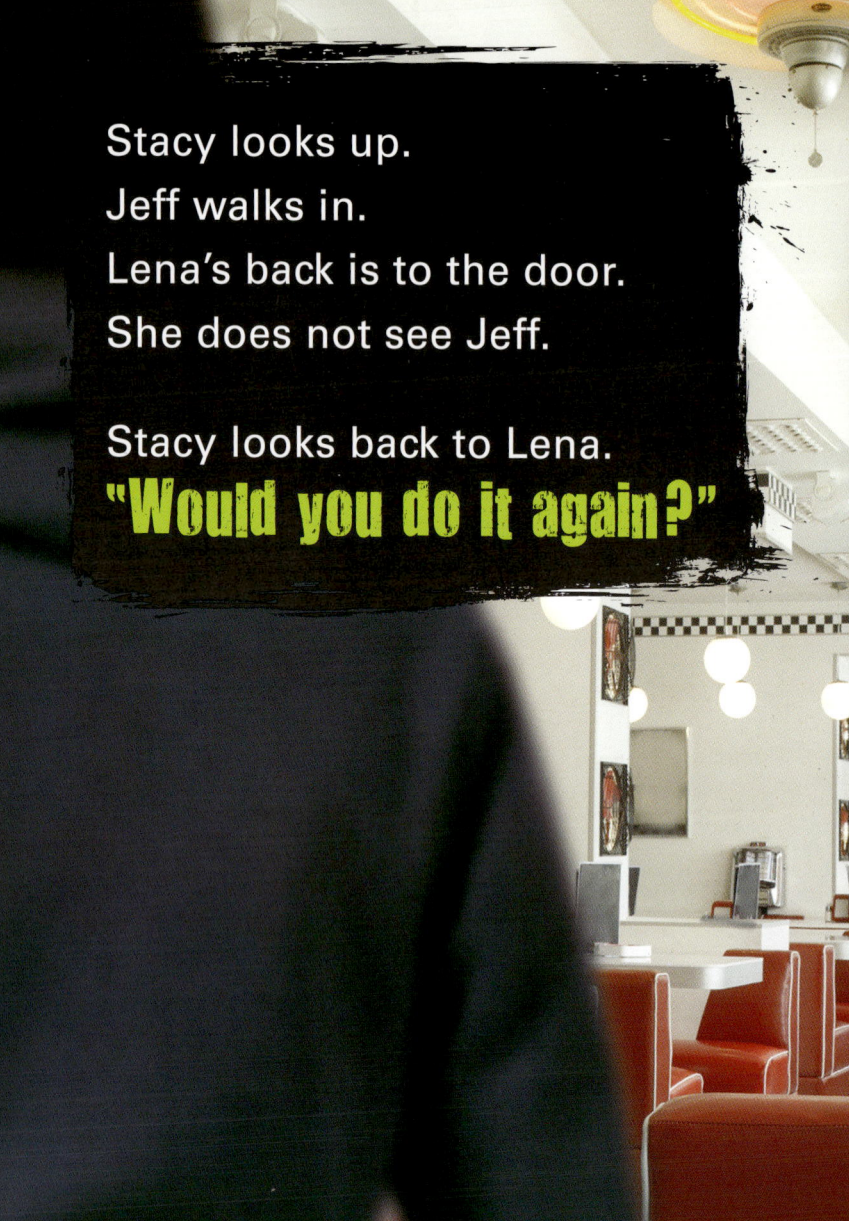

Stacy looks up.
Jeff walks in.
Lena's back is to the door.
She does not see Jeff.

Stacy looks back to Lena.
"Would you do it again?"

"Do what?"

"Go on another date with Jeff," Stacy says.

"I don't know," Lena says. "I like him. He's a great guy. But I don't know."

Stacy stands up. "Stay here. I'll be right back."

Stacy walks up to Jeff. "Lena told me about **your date.**"

Jeff shakes his head. "I don't know what happened."

"I know. We need to talk."
Stacy grabs Jeff's arm.
"Come with me," she says.

There is a store down the street.
Stacy takes Jeff there.

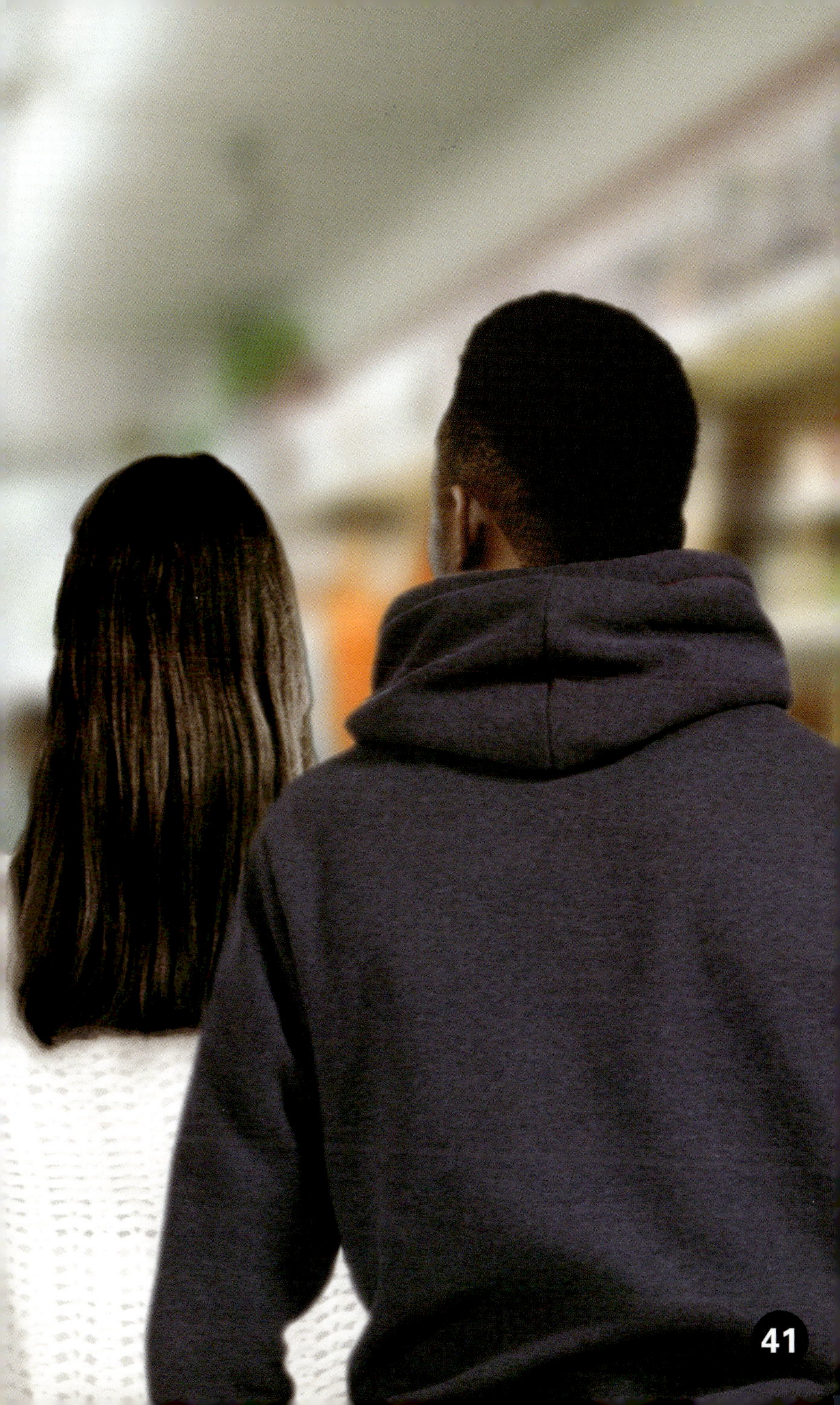

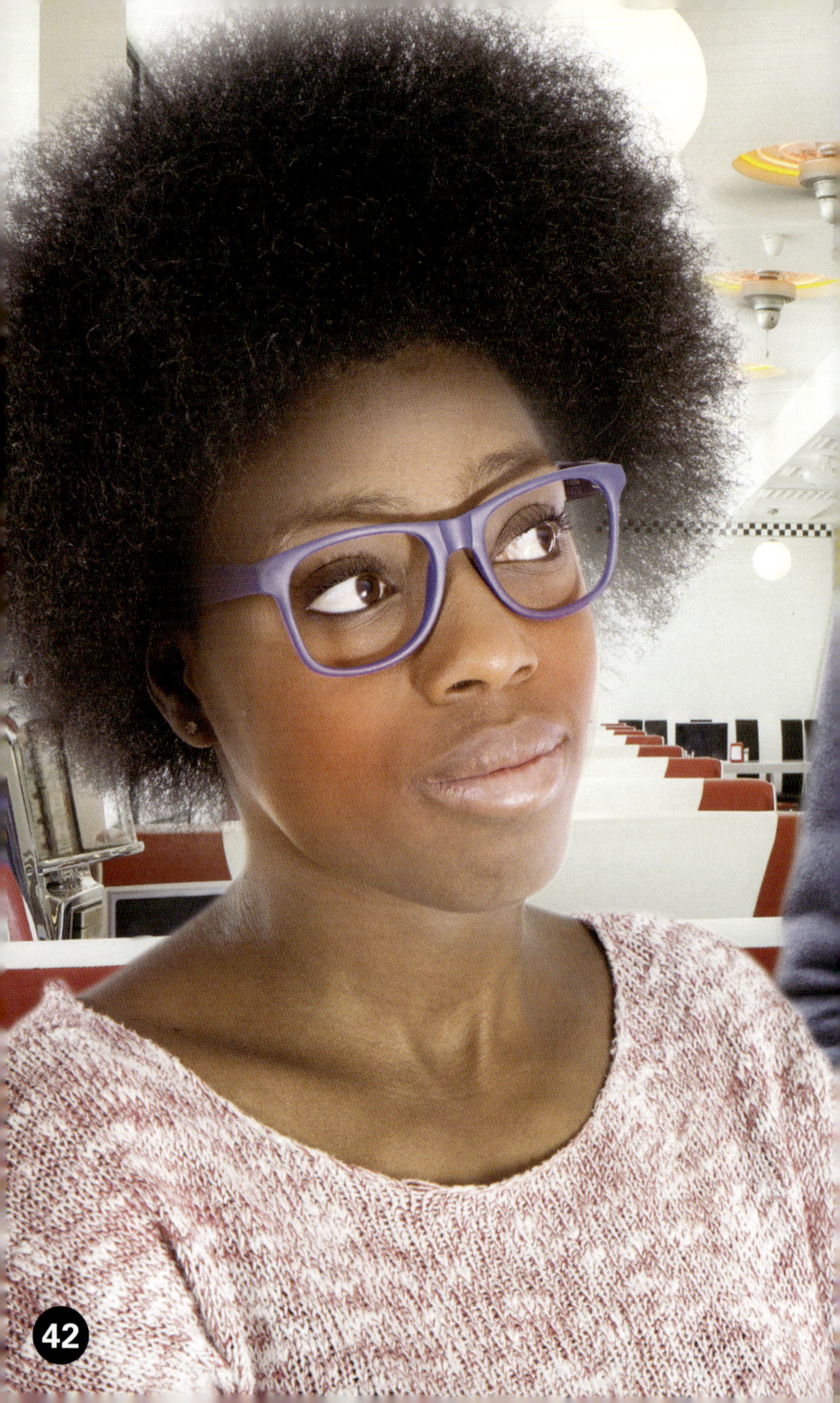

Lena looks around.
Stacy is gone.
"Where did Stacy go?"
Lena asks herself.

Stacy comes back with Jeff.
Lena sees them.
They walk up to Lena.
Her face turns **red.**

"Look who I found!"
Stacy says.

Jeff smiles at Lena.
"Hi," he says.

"Hi," Lena says.

Jeff sits down.
He puts a bag on the table.
Lena opens the bag.

45

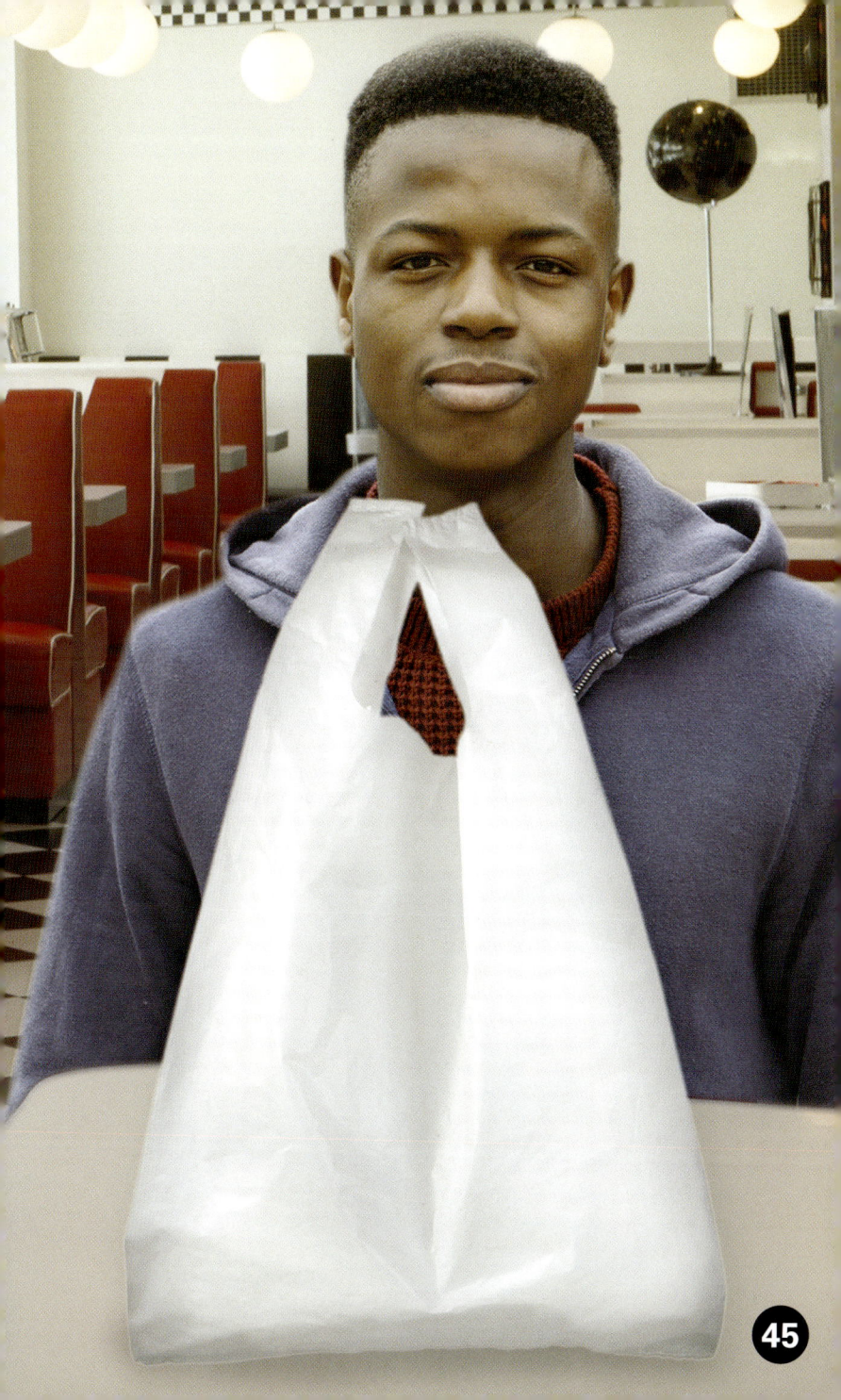

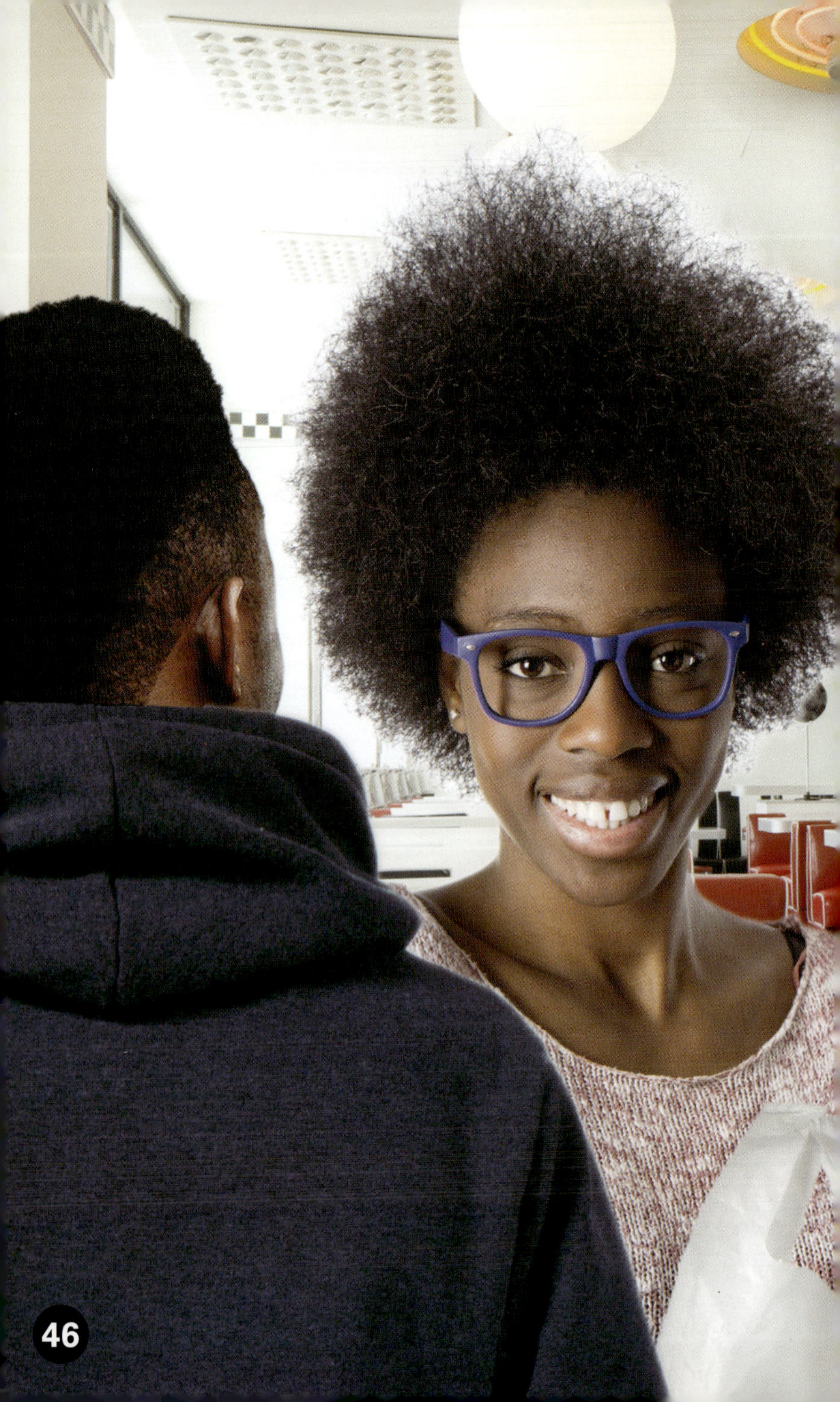

There is a bar of soap.
And a box of mints.

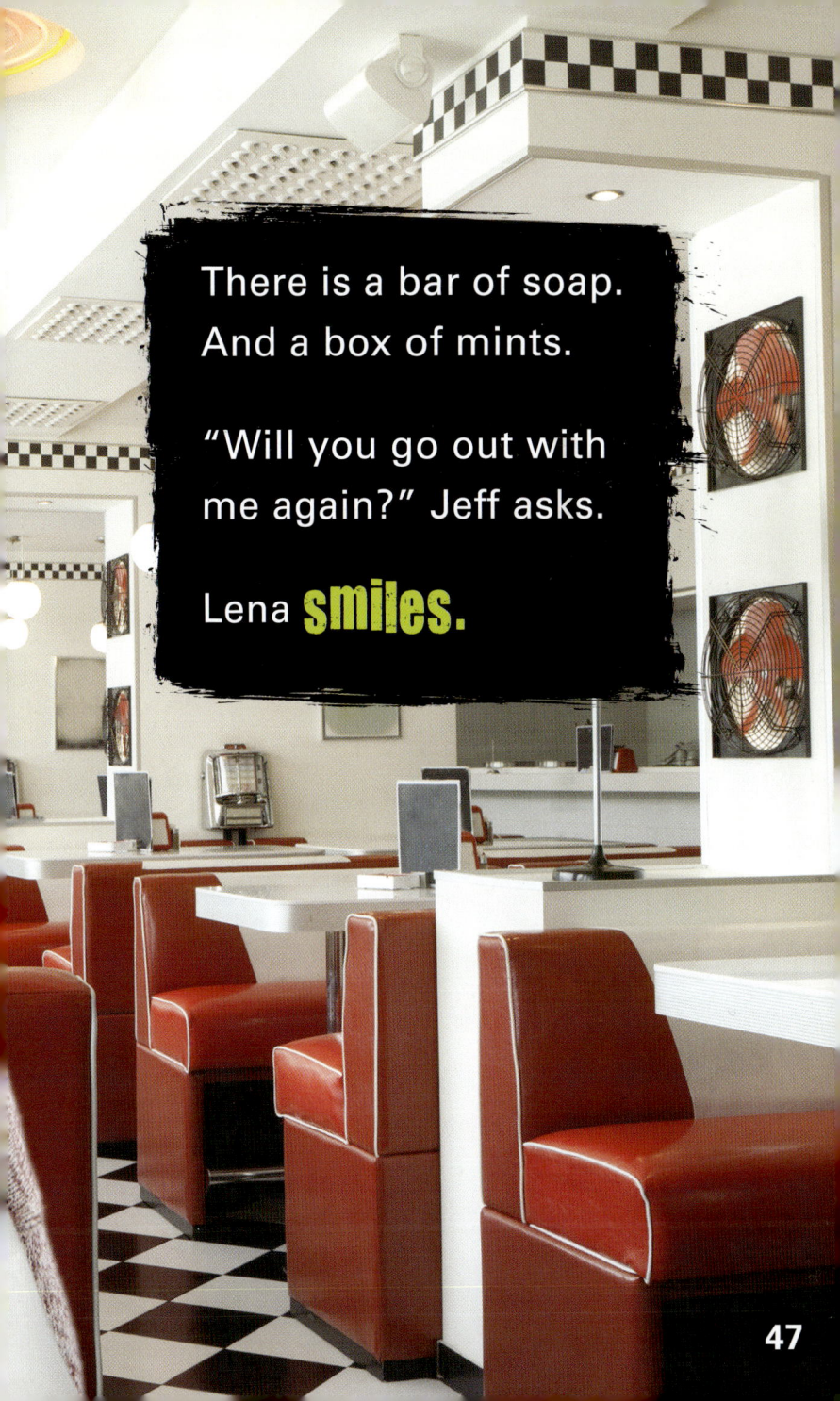

"Will you go out with me again?" Jeff asks.

Lena **smiles.**

48

TEEN EMERGENT READER LIBRARIES®
BOOSTERS

The Literacy Revolution Continues with New TERL Booster Titles!

Each Sold Individually

EMERGE [1]

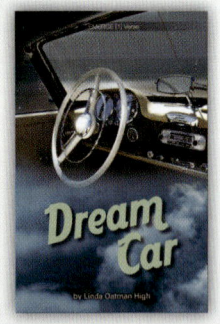

9781680211542

9781680211139

9781680211528

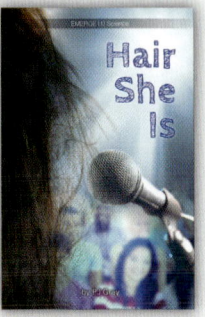

9781680211153

9781680211122

ENGAGE [2]

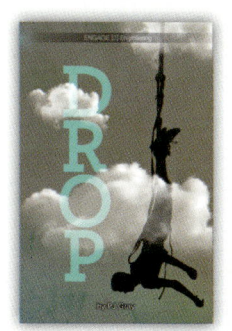

9781680211146

9781680211337

9781680211290

9781680211535

9781680211313

EXCEL [3]

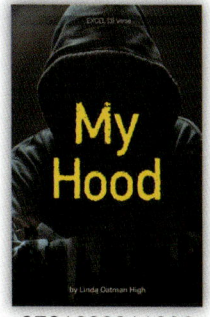

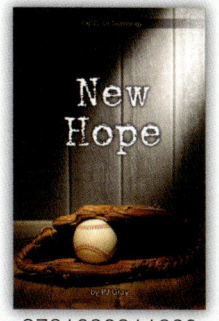

9781680211306

9781680211320

NEW TITLES COMING SOON!
www.jointheliteracyrevolution.com

[TERL]
TEEN EMERGENT READER LIBRARIES®

Our *Teen Emergent Reader Libraries®* have been developed to solve the issue of motivating the most struggling teen readers to pick up a book and start reading. Written at the emergent and beginning reading levels, the books offer mature, teen-centric storylines that entice teens to read.

[1] EMERGE
[2] ENGAGE
[3] EXCEL

| 9781622508662 | 9781622508679 | 9781622508686 |

www.jointheliteracyrevolution.com